T0194226

The House of the Broken Hands

Barbara O'Donnell

iUniverse, Inc.
Bloomington

The House of the Broken Hands

iUniverse books may be ordered through booksellers or by contacting:

iUniverse
1663 Liberty Drive
Bloomington, IN 47403
www.iuniverse.com
1-800-Authors (1-800-288-4677)

ISBN: 978-1-4620-1484-2 (sc)
ISBN: 978-1-4620-1485-9 (ebk)

Printed in the United States of America

iUniverse rev. date: 4/19/2011

Also by Barbara O'Donnell – available at celticgirlswriteon.com or pusheenpress@saclink.csus.edu

Novels – adult:

Love in an
Irish Circle
Lost Soul Child
The Town
Dream Walker
The White Bone Harp
Punky Rose Bagley
Alphabet for H Street

St. Francis Book Project – children's literature:

Eloise of St. Francis
Mary Alice, St. Francis, and the Wolf
Mrs. Mumble, Bumble, Grumble
Danny Dewberry and the Bully

Story Telling CD's:

The Black Rabbit Bar
Dooley Fagan
Memories from the Wild
A Christmas at St. Francis

VHS/CD:

So You Want to be a Writer

Memoir of a Friend:

Bram

To

My Grandma, Ione, a great story teller

Special Thanks

To Janine and Alan Harrington for their typing, editing, and technical work, and also for their advice about format of this bookeen.

Contents

Chapter 1

A Dark Old House

It is a beautiful 1900's Italianate house sitting on Poverty Ridge in Sacramento, California. Poverty Ridge has nothing to do with poverty. The area got the name when in the 1870's the rich began building their homes on this highest land east of the Sacramento River which flooded every year until the citizens built levees and weirs and dams. No. 10 is closed and empty. It's been this way for at least ten years. I walk the neighborhood and wonder about it.

The house is a large, imposing gray stucco, rectangular, two stories high with wide plate glass windows downstairs and upstairs. Drapes are drawn at the windows. On the cornices to each side of the upstairs windows, there are female muse's faces gazing down into the street. They smile as if contemplating a secret about the house. Wide brick steps lead to the front door which is massive. A small stone seat is built to one side of the door. A carefully manicured yard surrounds the house, not a blade of grass out of place, every flowering shrub carefully pruned and nurtured.

Other houses across the street are filled with families. People come and go. Lights are on at night, and cars are parked in driveways, but nothing moves at No. 10.

There is a similar mansion next door to No. 10 which is now the home of the McClatchy Library. I decided to consult the librarian. Yes, she said, the house was built about 1900 and had been empty for a long, long time, well as long as she could remember. Yes, this was Poverty Ridge, a joke produced by some wag when the expensive houses went up. And yes, she knew someone that could probably tell me about the house. That was Mrs. Gentry who had lived in the neighborhood all of her life. She resided, now, down the street at the Happy Retreat House, a euphemism for a convalescent hospital. Mrs. Gentry was as bright as a sapphire button, and if anybody could tell me about the house, she could.

I thanked the librarian and made my way to Happy Retreat House. I asked the receptionist if I could visit with Mrs. Gentry, and she called a nurse who listened to my request. She said that Mrs. Gentry would probably love company. She had few visitors these days since most of her friends had already gone to God, and her two sons lived in San Francisco. She ushered me into the parlor, and I was seated at a table. Eventually, the nurse wheeled Mrs. Gentry into the room. She was a bright-eyed, small chick of a woman. I introduced myself, and the nurse said she'd order tea for us.

"I live in the neighborhood," I told Mrs. Gentry. "I walk past No. 10 on 22nd Street, and I wonder about it. Nobody lives there. It's been dark for years. I was wondering if you could tell me anything about it. The librarian down the street said that you had lived in the neighborhood forever and might know the story." Just then an attendant brought us a tray of tea and cookies.

"Oh, yes," Mrs. Gentry smiled, "yes, I've lived here all my life over at No. 15, and Eve Duprey, the last of the Dupreys to live in the house, was my childhood friend. She told me many stories about that place. You see, there were two houses. The first one burned to the ground, and the lot sat empty for a long time before another was built. Eve inherited the family stories and the house," and she chuckled. "I told Eve that she should write all those stories down, but her hands were all twisted and her fingers had been badly broken. She said she couldn't write her own name hardly to say nothing of the stories.

I called it the House of the Broken Hands because of all those children that got their hands broke up at one time or another. Even the renters didn't last long. You see some property manager rented it out after Eve died, but they never stayed long, and the house would go empty again."

"And when did Eve die?" I asked.

"Oh, my, so many years ago. Now let's see," she said, thinking back, her eyes looking up to the ceiling in concentration. "Eve would have been about fifty, I'd imagine. She never married. She was a real recluse hardly ever going out of the house, and then one night, that old Chinese woman found her hanging in the cellar, belt around her neck. She was hanging from one of the cellar beams. That's what the police said. She got buried right away, and that old Chinese woman just disappeared after shutting up the house.

The house was empty forever, but finally a property manager, whoever that was I never knew, tried to rent it out. But nobody would stay for long in that house, and finally, it wasn't rented anymore."

"What stories did Eve tell you," I asked.

"Well, let me think where to begin. The family name was Duprey, Creoles from Louisiana as I remember her saying. After the Dupreys, there was the Jensens and the Heffstaters. Oh yes, and then there's the story of Mookie Sonnenberg.

The first renters were the Jensons, owned a bunch of shoe stores, if I remember right. They had a girl named Sarah. Well, Sarah came up with broken fingers on her right hand. Nobody knew what happened. She went to bed perfectly fine, and the next morning, she woke up with two of her fingers all twisted, purple, and swollen. Her mama took her right to the doctor who said they were broken, and he'd have to wrap them tight and have her mother apply ice on and off for a few days until the swelling went down, and then he'd have to cast them. When he asked what had happened, what kind of accident she had endured, her mother was vacant. She had no idea, and Sarah was mute on the subject.

But eventually, she told the story of the "lady." She said that a lady came into her room at night and sat on the end of her bed, and this one night, she had grabbed her hand and twisted her fingers. Mrs. Jenson said it was just a bad dream, but Sarah persisted in her story, and when a few weeks later, her other hand was hurt, the Jensons quickly moved out of the house.

And then there was the story of Mookie Sonnenberg. He was a mean boy, that Mookie. He went to the third grade with my son, Jessie. He bragged that he was going to get into that house after the Jensons left and go exploring, maybe pee all over the floor or break a chandelier. Mean boy, that Mookie. Well, sure enough he pried open a window one night. Sam Mason was with him, but Sam was scared to death once he got inside, and he says he huddled by the window. Mookie had brought some candle stubs and matches, and with a lighted candle he went up the big open stairway. Within a minute, he came running back down the stairs, screaming his head off, and both of those boys scrambled back through the window and went home.

Mookie never spoke again! His parents, doctors – nobody could figure out what was wrong with him. He looked perpetually astonished, and his mouth never quite closed again.

The house was empty for a long time then, but eventually, the Hoffstaters moved in. Mrs. Hofstater said she didn't believe the stories about the house, and besides she was having her priest bless it inside and out. But when her daughter came up with twisted, broken fingers, the Hoffstaters got out of there quick, I can tell you. I can't remember anyone living there after that."

Mrs. Gentry took a last sip of her tea. I could tell that all that concentrating had taken something out of her. "You must be getting tired," I said. "Perhaps, I can come another day, and we can talk some more."

"Surely," she smiled, "that would be nice. I'll try and remember Eve's stories, all those Duprey stories, those Creole Dupreys. Eve was so proud of that..." and her

Chapter 2

Narciste Duprey

Henri, Bess, and me! Lawd, lawd, what a family. Remembering back, it always been that way. From the first thing that I remember, we play together, we best friends. Couldn't act that way around the family sometime, but we knew it, knew it deep in our hearts. When peoples come to stay when we have big parties back there in Louisiana, I couldn't act like I have no truck with Henri and Bess. I have to be a lil old white gentleman, my maman tells me over and over. I'm ashamed by the way I lord it over Henri and Bess, commanding them to do this and that in front of aunts and uncles, or the neighbors down the road. But the minute those people gone, I can have my best friends back. We even talk about it; they say they understand and don't do nothing to get them or me in trouble.

Henri and Bess from two different families that live in the quarters. They born on the same day, and they like linked up together from that moment on. When they sixteen, they ask Papa two things… can they marry? And can they be my personal servants? That how we been living anyway, they taking care of me, so that don't cause no ruckus. Marrying? My papa say it probably time. They marry inside the church one afternoon. And that is a big thing, getting inside the church with a priest and everything, but my papa, he believe in that. By this time, my maman gone to God. I stood up beside Henri as the priest say I should do, and I vouch for him and for Bess. I was twenty-one years old.

Now my brother, Phillipe, he gona take over the land when my papa die. He already 'bout half running things. That's when I hear about gold discovered in California, and I ask papa's permission and blessing to go on out there. He say yes, and he agree that I can take Henri and Bess. Somebody gona dig for that gold and somebody gotta do for me. I have it in my head that I can stake a claim and just watch Henri dig them nuggets out of the earth. But it don't happen that way.

How it do happen is that by the time we sail around the Horn, land in San Francisco, and make our way up river to Sacramento, it 1850, California is a state, a free state. Henri and Bess, they free. But what we gona do? We ain't parting from each other. Claims is tuckered out as far as I can see. Don't want to go live up in the high mountains where the miners now do their digging and sluicing. What I note is that people need hardware and leather goods, saddles, and harnesses and such, and I meet a man that tell me how to buy low and sell high. He introduce me to a few people. Henri and me discuss a business proposition. I do the gla-handing and the books, and Henri, he make things just like he born to do on the

Louisiana land. We rent a store front and build us a small cabin behind it. Lawd, if papa could see me living with Henri and Bess, he about die. None of my family need to know nothing except I'm a businessman and making money.

A few years go by and a man get lonely to begin his own family. I get to asking around and a saloon keeper I know, he tell me about the Gomez family. Seems they an original Mexican family before the Mexicans get run off. They owned a lot of land at one time, but now they hardly get by, the sons hiring themselves out to run cattle and such. Got some daughters to marry off, so I get an introduction.

And that's how I meet Velvulotta. She a small, delicate, pretty woman. She have long black curls and big brown eyes, strange eyes, kinda glittery. She speak Spanish, French, and English. She haughty and proud, but I think you want that in a wife. So, I make a proposal to her papa, and he real happy to get her married to a businessman, and a Creole Catholic.

After we marry, I move into her papa's house, but I get it into my head that I will build a house up on Poverty Ridge, a fine house to show my station. So, that's what I do, and then I move Velvulotta into that house, and that's when the trouble start.

Chapter 2a

Velvulotta

I am not a brood sow. In my Mexican family, girls were to be married off. We didn't inherit the land, not an inch of it. Besides, my family had lost their land. There was nothing for anyone to inherit. But my father still considered it his duty to marry me off to a man with money and aspirations, and that's when he found Narciste Duprey, formerly of Louisiana, a second son, who had come to California to make his fortune. He was well on his way to achieving his goal.

Yes, he was tall, dark, and handsome, refined, educated, charming, just the kind of man my father would sell his daughter to. My timid mother considered this my only option. But I loathed the idea, loathed this man who would become my captor. I didn't want his offspring. I didn't care about his posterity. But I was forced to play a role, the lady of the gracious house. I produced an offspring, a boy, who I loathed as much as his father. I would not put that child to my breast. And one day when he came into my room filled with childhood exuberance, rushing to me to hug my frozen frame, out of annoyance I grabbed his hands, twisting, crunching, then I shoved him away. It was a small gesture in the big picture, but one that made my abhorrence quite clear.

Another child, another crunching. Leave me alone, my actions said to the inhabitants of the house, but then Narciste burned that house down, and I walked down the road.

Happiness? I only knew it briefly before the house burned down, and I was left with the memory of happiness as I nursed a third child.

Chapter 3

Bess

Mr. Narciste Duprey brings Henri and me to California in 1850, hoping to strike it rich. He come from a long line of Creole planters in Louisiana, but the first born, Mr. Phillipe, he inherit the family property, so when Mr. Narciste hear about the gold strike in California, he believe that he would try his luck. Henri and me, well, we belongs to Mr. Narciste, and he reckon that we should go with him which be fine with us. We sails from New Orleans around the Horn and gets to Sacramento just a month after California become a state, a free state. We don't belong to Mr. Narciste no more like our families been as long as we can remembers. But we three strangers in a strange land. So, we keeps together.

Mr. Narciste look around and see how hard prospecting is, and he see that the nearby hills be all played out already, so he look for another opportunity. He and Henri opens up a hardware and leather shop on

J Street. Now, Mr. Narciste, he don't get his hands dirty, of course, but my Henri, he a glory-filled blacksmith from the time he be a chile on the plantation. Duprey Smithy and Leathergoods do a good business. Mr. Narciste, he build a small house back of the store, and we shares it together. It is audacious, that what it be, a colored family and white man living together. But this here California. They no rules, no family, no neighbors spying on you, nobody telling you how to live. You do that practical or you get run over!

After a year or so, Mr. Narciste, he get it into his head that he need to build a big house up on the ridge and get himself a wife. So, he begin courting a girl named Velvulotta Gomez. Her family have a big rancheria in Yolo County but the Yanquees run them out. In Louisiana talk we say they lives in genteel poverty. They only too glad to marry Velvulotta off to a Creole businessman who speak French and be Catholic. So, the wedding happen.

We travels to Sonoma to find a priest who marries them. Takes a week of travel to get there and back. Henri and I does for the white folks on the trip, and I gets a good look at that girl. You can tell by their manners, the Gomezes, they seen better times, but that girl, that Velvulotta, I'm telling you there be something strange about that one. She pretty enough and petite. She have nice manners, and she speak Spanish and French, but well, I don't know, I just feels spooked in her presence. She never look right at you, but off to the side. And then when you don't pay her no mind, you gets this spooky feeling and the hairs on your neck rises up, and you looks around and finds her staring at you with her old ghost eyes.

That's what I tell Henri. I say "that girl have ghost eyes."

Well, now Mr. Narciste, he build a big house up on the ridge and move Ms. Velvulotta in. Henri and me builds a small cabin behind the house. I does the cooking for the family. Mr. Narciste, he hire a maid to do the cleaning and laundry. I run that house. Ms. Velvulotta take no truck with running a house and all.

Sometimes, she come into my kitchen to tell me that guests be coming for supper and to fix this or that. I listens and says, "Yes, ma'am," but after she leave, I always get the shivers. Sometime, I breaks a dish or drops a pot.

Mr. Narciste begin treating Velvulotta as if she a piece of the furniture. It her fault. She don't talk, don't say nothing to nobody 'cept to give orders once in awhile. When Mr. Narciste have his business friends to supper, Ms. Velvulotta sit at the head of the table, but she hate it. And when supper over, Ms. Velvulotta go to her room. Mr. Narciste, he try to talk to her, but she just sit there looking at him with them strange eyes.

Now, Mr. Narciste, he want children. Henri and me, we already has a boy. I hears Mr. Narciste and Ms. Velvulotta arguing about having a chile. He say he want family, and she say she no breed sow. Somehow, he overcome because one day he announce Ms. Velvulotta with chile. It is about this time that he get himself a "café au lait" woman the other side of town, and he keep her just fine.

Ms. Velvulotta have a boy, Little Narciste, we calls him. And Mr. Narciste, he brings a bottle of wine down to Henri, and them two gets drunk, I can tell you. Mr.

Narciste say "the line go on." And Henri, he say "it sure do and all."

But two days after they celebrate, I know something wrong. That chile don't thrive, and finds out why. The maid take the chile to Ms. Velvulotta to nurse, but the minute her back be turned, Ms. Velvulotta lay that chile down and let him squall. I has milk from my Thomas, so I wet nurse that chile even sleeping on a pallet in the kitchen to nurse him at night.

I tells Mr. Narciste everything, how Ms. Velvulotta don't take care of that chile, how a chile have to be held, and loved-up, and fed or there be no more chile! Mr. Narciste, he tell me he grateful, and he always remember how I takes care of his son. And you knows he never buy something for Little Narciste, but he buy the same for Thomas too. And when he get a tutor to school Little Narciste, he say my Thomas must be tutored too. Mr. Narciste a good man, a good man.

Ms. Velvulotta takes to her room more and more now. She write in a little book, and she say her prayers, and she reads books she order from the new library. She even want her meals brung up to that room. I thinks she go crazy sitten in that room every day, watching out the window. Henri, he say she already crazy.

It be about this time that Little Narciste, he come screaming into the kitchen with his hand all out of shape, his fingers nearly twisted off. I plunges his hand into the cold water pail and sends the maid running down to Henri's shop to get him home. Mr. Narciste, he come running and take Little Narciste to the buggy where Henri wait to get him to the doctor. When we asks him what happen, all he say is maman, maman. He never go to her room again even to kiss her goodnight as his papa want him to do.

Then Ms. Velvulotta hav'en another baby. How this happen, I sure don't know. I tell Henri it must be a miracle of the Lord. Little Anna be born, and I finds a wet nurse for her right away. Ain't tak'en no chances with this chile!

It was the summer that Anna turns two years old that Mr. Narciste get it into his head to enlarge the house. That be a terrible mess, I tells you, with workers coming and going, and the noise, dirt, walls be torn down, the roof remodeled. But there was one room in the house where nobody disturb. Workmen say Ms. Velvulotta give you the evil eye, and then terrible things happen. Like what happen to Old Pike. Old Pike, he a carpenter, and one day he have to measure something in Ms. Velvulotta's room. He open the door, and there she sit on her chamber pot! Old Pike run like the devil, and he don't come back for three days. But the day he do come back, he climb on the roof, fall, and break his neck and die. Most of the workmen quits right away, and Mr. Narciste, he have a hard time getting that house finished.

It right after the house get back to normal that I wake up one night hearing a woman's laugh and grunting animal sound. I gets out of bed and looks out the window to my back garden where the noise be coming from. I know what be going on. A couple lay in the grass under one of the apple trees making the beast. I can't help watching, trying to figure out who it be? Then, there be a "whoop" and a woman in a white flowing nightgown untangle herself, shake herself off, and slink toward the big house. Jesus, Mary, and Joseph! It be Ms. Velvulotta.

Night after night, this bad thing go on, and I finally decides to see who the man be. I takes the bat that Henri keep by his side, and I goes out and circles around the garden fence, outside where they be. I looks over, and whada you think I sees? Sun Wang, the Chinese gardener, he pulling up his pants. Ms. Velvulotta go for the house, and Sun Wang hoist himself up over the fence only to land right beside where I stands with that bat. "You gets away and never comes back," I tells him, "or I tells Mr. Narciste everything." He run like all the imps of hell be after him.

Ms. Velvulotta go to that place night after night, and she call for Sun Wang. Then she sit under that tree, and she cry and cry.

"Damn Chinee gardener," Mr. Narciste say to me, "he don't come no more. Where he at?"

"Can't count on Chinese," I tells him, "better hire a nice Italian man, an old man that takes care of your property nice."

Then Anna get bad twisted fingers in the middle of the night. I hears her scream from the big house, and I runs to find her room a mess, everything smashed and teared up, and that little girl standing there shrieking with twisted, broken fingers. Mr. Narciste, he with his café au lait woman, but I gets Henri to go for the doctor.

The next day when Mr. Narciste find out what happen, he tells me to keep the children at my cabin. About midnight, several dray wagons and horses come to the house, and workers carry everything of value out and takes it away. Next thing you know, that house on fire, and we watches it burn to the ground. Mr. Narciste take his children and his café au lait family to San Francisco after that. The last I seen of Ms. Velvulotta, she walking down the road with a carpet bag.

Little Narciste and Anna come on the train sometime. They stay at the Crombie Hotel. Miss Anna always wear gloves and never take them off. We love their visit. Feel like they our own children.

About ten years go by when I shopping on K Street. I looks across the street at this old-fashioned, bedraggled woman. She carry a market basket in one hand, and she hold onto a Chinese girl with the other. That girl be 'bout ten years old. The woman look my way, and I gets that spooky feeling all over me, for if it doesn't be Ms. Velvulotta herself. And that Chinee girl, she have her hand all bandaged up. Ms. Velvulotta move on in a hurry, and I watches her go into a low-life hotel. I sends Henri the next day to ask for her. I like the curious cat after all these years, but the man at the desk say no woman describe like that live at that hotel, and no Chinee girl allowed there. I never sees her again.

Chapter 4

Little Narciste

Papa always said that land could be haunted, that spirits who couldn't find eternal rest prowled about at the scene of their torture, crimes, or just bad luck. And papa said that the lot at Number Ten on Twenty-Second Street in Sacramento was just that sort of place. He told me not to build a house on that lot, but I didn't listen to him. I wanted independence for myself, and most of all for Anna. She was scared of her own shadow.

I worked in my father's business in San Francisco, but when Henri and Bess both died in Sacramento, and when their son wasn't interested in working in the leather and tool company Henri and my father had made famous, I asked papa if I could take over that facility. He agreed, but when I told him that I wanted to build a house on the Twenty-second Street property, he began talking about the evil that had been done there. He suspected that my mother's ghost hovered over that land.

My mother! How can I explain my mother? She was cold, reclusive, and downright mean. She twisted my fingers breaking them when I was a small child, and I never forgot or forgave. And then the same thing happened to Anna. That's when papa moved us to San Francisco and burned down the house.

The last time I saw my mother, she was walking down the street, a heavy cloak thrown over her nightgown. I watched her go feeling relieved. I never wanted to see her again, and I never did. Well, not in that form anyway.

My papa and his Charlotte were very kind and generous to Anna and me. We had a fine growing up. Papa said his people back in Louisiana would have a fit if they knew that his white children were being raised by a café au lait woman, but then come to think of it, hadn't he and his brothers, and generations of Dupreys been raised by black nannies? About the only difference was that those children didn't live in the cabins or New Orleans houses of the black women. They lived in the big house, and the black women came to them. Papa said there wan't much difference that he could reckon.

And so that's how I came to move Anna and myself to Sacramento, take over the Duprey Tool and Die Company, and build the Italianate house on papa's property.

It was a beautiful, big spacious house made of the finest materials by gifted craftsmen.

Anna was a fine house mistress and hostess for my formal dinner parties for business associates. And I saw to it that she always had enough servants to do the literal work. Anna always wore lace gloves to hide her crooked, arthritic fingers. She was very embarrassed about her hands and made sure that nobody ever saw them.

We had only lived in the house a few months when she lost her gloves. She had taken them off and laid them on her bedside table, and the next morning, they were gone. She hunted everywhere. Had they somehow slipped behind the table? Were they under the bed? Gotten tangled in the bedclothes? Had she reached out for them in her sleep, perhaps having one of her bad dreams about mother twisting her fingers? Had she sleepwalked, perhaps, moving the gloves? She counted the additional pairs of gloves in her bureau drawer. There were five. Altogether she had six pair. So, where was the pair she had taken off before going to bed?

No one had been in the house that night except me. Sometimes, when we entertained and it was a long night, one of the maids like Brige would sleep in the kitchen rather than going home in the middle of the night. But on this night, no one had slept over. We discussed the strange phenomena over breakfast. We couldn't fathom the mystery of it all.

And then Brige, the breakfast cook at that time, overheard our conversation as she came into the room with plates of bacon and eggs. She listened intently as she poured our tea, and then quietly, she said almost to herself, "Maybe the lady took them."

Immediately, Anna's eyes opened wide as she turned to look at Brige, and chills began at the base of my neck and shivered down my back.

"What lady?" I asked, hoping that it was some kind of old Irish expression, perhaps a joke.

Brige stood up very straight and looked from Anna to me. "The lady that prowls about the place," she said matter-of-factly.

"What are you talking about?" I now asked getting annoyed. "The only lady in this house is Anna, our invited guests, and you maids."

"Yes, Sir," Brige said attending to the teapot.

"Then what are you talking about?" I insisted again.

"Well, Sir, it must be my Irish imagination," she said smiling as if to placate me. "It's nothing, Sir."

She left the room. I looked at Anna and shrugged. Anna delicately sipped her tea, but she had a worried look on her face. "Ma Cher," I said lovingly, "don't listen to servants' gossip. Your gloves will show up in some unexpected place, and you'll just laugh about all of this."

Anna looked at me very seriously. "Servants' gossip is the only thing to listen to," she said. "Charlotte taught me that."

Chapter 5

Narciste

I tole Little Narciste not to build a house on that lot on Poverty Ridge, but he won't listen to me. He insist on going to Sacramento after Henri and Bess die to run the business. He say Anna go with him. Anna, she don't go to school, hardly ever go to church, never make friends, her only close connection, Little Narciste.

He build a new style house, not Victorian, but Italianate. It's a big, solid house, rooms big enough for a family of share croppers, three generations long, to live there. On one side is a parlor, and on the other side is a library. Behind the library a music room, and behind the parlor, a dining room. At the back, got a kitchen big enough for a hotel, I swear. Upstairs, six bedrooms, walk-in closets, and two bathrooms with hot and cold running water. Little Narciste, he spare no money in building this house. It have the finest woods, tiles, chandeliers, and silver door knobs. Fancy and beautiful. Good thing I make so much money in my lifetime. All my children like fancy things, just like my family in Louisiana always do.

I visit them, but I feel something, like Velvulotta's old ghost eyes still on me. And when Anna tell me that she see a little Chinee girl in the alley behind the property every day, just sitting in the weeds under an apple tree that used to be Bess's garden, it gives me the shivers, and I take the train home to San Francisco and Charlotte.

I never tole you about Charlotte. She my real wife all these years. The men in my family, we always have two marriages. One official and bring about the next generation. One for pleasure and real love, and that mean keeping a café au lait woman in New Orleans. Everybody understand how things are done, and that is that. We send our café au lait children to the finest schools in France if a boy, and settle our girls with rich planters who agree to certain conditions. Our cafe au lait families set free in the end, unless we get drunk and killed in a fight or bit by a water moccasin in the swamps trying to catch a poacher on our land. We have lawyers draw up freedom papers.

I need a marriage with an old respected family for my business and posterity, but after I get that settle, I look around for a woman for my heart and I find it in Charlotte. Well, I guess that neither family relationship turn out like I expect.

Velvulotta Gomez is from a fine, old family, but nobody in this new California care. They see them Mexicans as conquered people. Those white boys from the Northeast don't care if the Gomezes at one time owned thousands of acres, that they have fine manners, speak Spanish and French, are cultured and well educated. No, they just Mexicans who don't count. The family is very happy to marry Velvulotta off to me, a man in business with a French background and manners. They never think they have such a chance, particularly because of Velvulotta's personality. It said that the beautiful Velvulotta inherit her grandmother's eyes, and they are eyes that can see right into the soul of people. They are eyes of great power. They are eyes that come from another important woman in the family. She a native born woman. She have high standing in the tribe and is trained by a shaman. A Gomez man see her, fancy her, catch her, rape her, and rope her up and bring her back to his hacienda. She a prisoner in the servant's quarters, but at night, she pace like a wild animal, determine to escape. The Gomez visit her often, compel her to couple with him. Servants hold her down. Eventually she become with child and deliver a baby girl. The Gomez not pleased. He need sons. He say she give him a girl on purpose, and now he get rid of her, but before he let her go, he come upon her one black night without servants to hold her down, and in their struggle, she thrust a knife into the hollow of his throat and make her escape.

The baby girl brought up by the Gomez family. Nobody ever talk about what happened, but everyone aware that the chile have her mother's eyes, and they afraid of her. Those eyes show up again in Velvulotta several generations later, and with the eyes come some strange power.

Velvulotta have a strange power all right. She compliant enough at first, but it isn't long that I learn how awful those eyes can be. I never feel comfortable in her bed. After coupling, I have to get away. I dream she hold a small jeweled dagger in her hand, and she plunge it into my throat while I sleep.

She charming enough to my business associates, but she make them feel nervous too, I can tell, and everyone feel better when she excuse herself after supper and leave us to our brandy and cigars. And after Little Narciste born, I stay away from her for awhile. She retreat into her bedroom and rarely come out. And thank heaven for Bess or there be no Little Narciste. And then come the day she twist his fingers real bad.

I was furious about that. I storm into her room and tole her that if she ever hurt that chile again, I kill her. She just lay on the bed with glittery eyes looking at me, and then as I fume and pace, she untie her dressing gown and lay it back that I see her nakedness, her beautiful white breasts with cherry dark nipples, her generous soft belly, and the mound of black hair between her legs with a musky smell that come to me right across the room. She begin to undulate her hips and spread her legs open, all the while looking at me with those awful eyes. But it put a trance on me, for sure, and before I know it, I have my cock out of my pants, and I pushing it into her and rocking as fast as I can. When that silver rush from my cock, I yell so loud that I know Bess and Henri hear it in their cabin behind the house. Then, as I roll over on the bed, she get up, fasten her dressing gown, turn, and hiss at me like a cat. I fly out of that room, I can tell you, and I never go back. That's when I seeded Anna.

And you know the rest of the story. After Anna's fingers twisted and broken, I have everything packed out of that house, and I set it on fire myself. Evil got right into the walls, and there is only one way to get rid of it. I wish

Velvulotta burn up with it, but she just watch silently as everything crated and taken out. Then she pack a carpet bag, throw a cloak over her nightdress and walk out of the house and down the road without saying one word. The kitchen already on fire.

I don't know where she go. Her family either dead or back in Mexico. She have no one in Sacramento. I don't care. I never hear from her. I never receive so much as a letter from a lawyer. I just collect my insurance money and move my two families to San Francisco where I now have additional business interests.

I hire men to clean up the debris from the fire, and the lot just sit there as other houses are built around it, that is until Little Narciste get it into his head to build his own house. I tole him not to do it, but he won't listen. But he find out. Oh yes, he find out.

Chapter 6

Narciste

Today I think about my love. Charlotte my big café au lait woman. I meet her in a brothel down on Front Street. That place call Moonsong, a nice place where you go to have a drink and play cards and relax with other gentlemen; it a high-up place, and the girls beautiful. Charlotte a new girl. She pour wine into my glass as I play cards and speak to me in a New Orleans accent. After I take her upstairs, she say her planter gentleman gone and die on her after only two years, and he leave her nothing. She sell the contents of the house he keep before his regular family descend on her, and she has enough to buy passage on a ship to California. Of course, she not free to go, but the family lawyer take pity on her and help her make her escape. He say the papers all drawn up for her freedom-to-come, but the man die before they get signed and filed properly.

She gets as far as Sacramento before her money run out, and she take shelter, really, in the Moonsong. The madam good to the girls, and the clients "gentlemens." And she get a fair share of the money unlike some of the places where the poor girls owe more at the end of the week than they take in.

Charlotte a big girl the color of café au lait. She an inch taller than me, big boned, big bosomed, big assed, everything big. She has a beautiful face, a sweet face, a dainty face unexpected because of the bigness of the rest of her. I want her to be my woman and ask for her favor. The madam don't want to lose her, but she know when a girl want to move on, and you make it difficult, she won't be good with the customers anyway.

I move her into a small house in Alkalie Flats, a few blocks from the river. It a little lacy Queen Anne cottage with room for a garden out back. And I see to it that she dressed like a queen, have the best furniture, linens, china, crystal, and silver. I hire a maid to do the cleaning, cooking, and washing. All Charlotte have to do is please me and be my companion, and she does it well. I love to be at her house, be her special man, be rub and lather in the big tub in the bathroom which has running water. She see to it our meals are the best, our wine from France, my cigars Cuban, and she a great reader from the daily newspapers to the best of books. She discuss anything from politics to philosophy. And in bed, she about do me in. She trained to this kind of life, and she superb at the job.

As things between peoples is, we have three children together. Renee, a daughter just like her mother, Francoise, a big, hardy boy who pass for white. Then there James, a throw back, black boy, who look like he came right out of Africa. His mother don't consider him "right" and he knows it and he rebel, gamble, split heads, get drunk and lay in the gutter, and finally I put him on a ship to Chile where he is to work at one of my farms. Renee, I marry off real good, and Francois go to school in France. We proud of these children.

When I move the families to San Francisco after the fire, I live openly in a Victorian house on Church Street. This a new era in California where nobody care who you are or what you do, long as you don't flaunt it too much. Narciste, Anna, and my café au lait children grow up together, and Charlotte a good maman to Narciste and Anna.

Narciste's hand heal well. You never know that his fingers get all broken. But Anna's look crippled, and Charlotte make sure that Anna always wear pretty lace gloves to hide the fact. "Ma Cher," she tell her, "your hands look prettier wearing this lace. Don't worry your fingers aren't straight."

Chapter 7

Anna

I came to Sacramento with Little Narciste. He was good to me all my life. When the lady first appeared, he said I'd been listening to too many stories told in the kitchen by our Irish maid, Brige, but that wasn't it at all. It was shortly after my lace gloves went missing. I took them off only at night, and I put them on my bedside table. In the morning, they were gone. A second pair went missing a few days later, so I got to putting them under my pillow. Brige and I talked about the lady that she saw prowling about the house. Brige said she was rarely in the kitchen, but she saw her upstairs when she went to make up the beds and tidy the rooms.

But I did worry, and then came the night that I saw her too. And once I saw her, I knew who she was. It was our maman. Even though I was a small child when our father moved us away from that place, I instantly knew who the spirit was. Yes, it was maman. I would wake up, and she would be standing at the foot of my bed just looking at me. She always wore a long white nightgown, and her hair hung down around her shoulders. Her eyes were so strange, glaring-like. At first, it frightened me to death, and I called out for Narciste, who came into the room and sat beside me on the bed, and said it was just a bad dream. He couldn't see a thing.

But she came again and again. Brige said to get all my courage and ask her what she wanted? And that might make her go away. And it did for awhile. Yes, I sat right up and said in a solid voice I didn't feel, "What do you want?" She didn't answer at all. She dropped a pair of my lace gloves on the foot of the bed and just vanished. But a few months later, she came back.

"What do you want!" I demanded time and time again. But she never replied. I didn't want to worry Narciste anymore, so I only confided in Brige, and it got so she didn't frighten me at all.

"Look what you did to my hands!" I told her one night, holding them up in a shaft of moonlight that came through the window. "Why did you do this to me?" And then I started to cry. At that, she left. So from then on, when she appeared, I just held out my hands to her, and she'd get agitated, but she'd leave.

It was the night, the awful night of the Christmas party, that Narciste came across her outside his bedroom on the landing. Narciste, he loved Christmas, and he demanded that we decorate the house, top to bottom. The second Christmas that we'd been in the house, it was decorated as usual, and Narciste, he had a big party. Everybody who had a name at all was invited. A small orchestra played in the parlor, and the dining room table was abundant in platters of meats and cheeses, baskets of breads and pastries, and bowls of fresh fruit. In the center was a big wassail bowl, and a bar was set up on the sideboard. And oh the grand ladies that came in their Christmas finery, and the gentlemen! The merry gentlemen.

I was so shy, really, although Narciste said that I had come out of my shell a lot. But I would have liked to peek through the kitchen door to watch the people and festivities, but of course, I had to stand in the foyer and greet the guests and watch over the table to be sure that as soon as a platter emptied, it was filled again.

The neighbors had been invited in, and one of them was that beautiful Evelyn girl. She lived at Number Fifteen, and she was fifteen. There is some synchronicity in that. She came with her parents and a younger sister, and she was all gussied up, as Brige would say. She wore a fine, rose silk dress, and her hair was swept up on top of her head. Many of the men were doing her honor, I can tell you, especially after their glasses had been filled a few times. But Narciste seemed enchanted as if she was the queen of the faeries as Brige would say. And he hovered about her all night. I was busy with the table, and I didn't see her parents and sister leave. But at one point, late into the night, I noted that they were gone but she wasn't. I thought it very odd. But eventually, the party drew down, the musicians packed up and left and the servants began cleaning up.

I went upstairs to retire. Since I saw a light under Narciste's door at the opposite end of the hall, I knew he was still up, and I knocked. I wanted to say that it was a wonderful party, and hadn't everything gone beautifully?

But Narciste turned off his light at my knock, and he said in a tired voice that he was exhausted. We could talk in the morning. So, I went off to bed, but I couldn't sleep well, I was so keyed up after our grand event.

About 4:00 a.m., I heard a commotion in the hall and crept out of bed to spy. That's when I saw that beautiful girl all bedraggled now coming out of Narciste's room, shoes in hand, and staying close to the wall and handrail of the stairs begin her descent down the servants' stairs. I saw through his door that she hadn't closed all the way, probably so as not to make any noise. Narciste was snoring away in the bed. I went back to my room scandalized from the top of my head to the tips of my toes. And that's when the lady appeared outside his door and began a high pitched laughing which awakened Narciste. When I got to the hallway to spy on the proceedings once more, I saw her clearly, heard that terrible laugh, and saw Narciste standing in the doorway a few feet from her with the hair raised up on the top of his head.

Chapter 8

Chinee Girl

I was about thirty years old when my mama and I watched that house being built. For years, my mama and I lived homeless, rough, down by the river, or on the back of that lot. At the back where gardens had once been, it was overgrown with wisteria and honeysuckle, making canopies between the trees. Hedges had grown tall as trees. It was a forest fairyland, a place where a woman and girl could build a camp and not be bothered or observed.

Once some boys spied on us, probably had been playing hide and seek. We made makeshift bundles and hurried away back down to the river. "Led 'em go," I heard one boy say, "they just bums."

My mother told me stories about the fine house that once had stood on this lot, about the man who lived there and his terrible children, but she never put herself into the picture. As I got older, I wondered how she knew so much, but any time that I would ask a question, she would look at me with her strange eyes that gave me the shivers, and I'd clam up like I was suppose to.

Like the time I asked her why I was Chinee and she wasn't. By this time, I knew about men and women. I'd seen things in the river groves. She never answered me, but turned away with a strangling sound, made the signal that I wasn't to follow her, and left me for three days. I never asked that question again.

We watched the diggers and the builders as they began to lay out that new house. My mother noted the man who gave the orders, curled her lip at him and softly cursed. It was like she had known him in the past. And as the house grew, my mother began to shrink. Each day, she seemed less and less until one day she was just a shadow who slipped between the cracks of the cellar bricks before they got cemented up.

One thing I was good at was making things grow. Ever since I was a girl, I had planted things. I'd collect seeds from the vegetables we found out behind the restaurants where we scavenged. I'd find a place down by the river or on the old lot to make a garden. I don't know how I knew what to do. It just came natural. And sometimes, we'd stay in a place long enough to harvest what I had planted. That was the best part.

I was careful after my mama slipped away not to be observed. I was afraid that gardeners would reclaim the back of the lot, and after people moved into the finished lot, that's what happened. I'd taken my bundle and moved on, but each twilight, I'd come back to see the progress. Gardeners like me, Chinee, they trimmed and hauled away brush, raked and pruned. But the best part was when they began to plant a rose garden, then vegetables, then fruit trees.

I had a terrible urge to join them which finally gave me an idea, and the courage to carry it out. With my bundle over my shoulder, I approached the back door and knocked. A friendly Irish woman came to the door. I told her I was looking for work. I could do about anything, especially working in gardens. I didn't need no wages. I'd work for room and board. I knew what room and board was from the times when mama could afford to stay in boarding houses, helping out in the kitchens.

But those times didn't last long since mama didn't know much about kitchen work and besides she always scared people. Then, we'd go back to living rough, but I longed for those times curled up on a real cot at night with a roof over my head. The Irish woman, Brige, she just smiled at me and said she'd been watching the garden being conceived. Conceived. She said conceived, just like a living thing was coming to life, which, of course, it was. She'd seen me watching too. A yellow cat came up then, and he rubbed against my shins. Brige said that was a good sign. She'd talk with Miss Anna. Lord knew they could use some help. I should come back the next day.

And that's how I came to live in the house, way down deep next to the root cellar. There was a little alcove where they fixed me up a cot, a wash stand, and a few shelves for my things. I had a basin and pitcher for water and a chamber pot which I carefully emptied outside beyond the garden each morning, burying any trace of myself.

I felt mama's spirit real close, and sometimes I would wake up in the night thinking that her glittery eyes had been looking at me, her breath on my cheek.

Now Mr. Narciste lived in the house, and Brige told me to keep out of his sight until Miss Anna made things right. So that's the way I lived for several months, doing work for the household like polishing silver, and when Mr. Narciste was gone, working in the garden. The Chinee men still came every week.

Those Chinee men, they just looked at me, and they talked in their own language about me, I could tell. But I stayed aloof from them, gesturing with my hands about the way I should do something. One kindly, old man, he took a special interest in me, looked at the small gold ring I wore on my right hand, about the only thing that my mama had given me. He'd study me real hard, then he'd pat my shoulder and make signs that I did well in the garden. He would nod and nod, and one time his eyes filled up with tears. Some of those younger men would look at me sideways, but I ignored them.

I hadn't been in the house long before there was a big kerfluffle, as Anna said. A neighbor came to the house one night, and there was yelling, and the pounding of a fist on the table, and then Miss Anna, she was crying, and Brige slammed things around the kitchen.

Then Brige, she tell me there was to be a wedding. Mr. Narciste and that neighbor girl, that Evelyn. Miss Anna did the house up real nice, and a priest came and married Mr. Narciste and that girl right in the living room. I peered at the goings on from the kitchen door where I helped Brige. The girl's family was there and a few other people. The men got drunk, and then the people left, and that girl looked as sad as can be.

The next thing you knew, Brige said there was going to be a baby in the house, and it was time to tell Mr.

Narciste they needed more help and that she knew a Chinee girl who would be a good servant. And that's when she introduced me to Mr. Narciste. Miss Anna stood to one side looking really concerned. She told Mr. Narciste she wanted me hired, and so that's how I came to be a part of the household and didn't have to hide anymore. I still lived in the little alcove in the cellar rather than in the servants' room with Brige. I liked it that way; and I felt I was near mama.

Mr. Narciste was gone much of the time, even more than before he was married. And that girl, Evelyn, got downright fat before that baby came. She and Miss Anna seemed to get along fine, and they spent many an afternoon knitting baby things, or appliquéing kittens or puppies on baby gowns. Evelyn hardly ever left the house. Miss Anna seemed her only friend. Once in awhile, her mother came calling "tsking" about this and that. Brige and me, well, we didn't like her at all.

And then that baby came in the middle of the night, almost got born before the doctor got to the house. That baby was a girl, and Miss Anna said her name should be Eve, kinda a shortened version of her mother's name. Mr. Narciste, he looked like he didn't know what to do with that baby. He just kinda stared at her as if he couldn't figure out where she came from. But that baby had three mothers between Evelyn, Miss Anna, and Brige. Evelyn dressed that baby up like a doll, and Miss Anna read to her for hours, and that baby seemed to listen to her voice as if she understood every line of those stories.

And then one night when I was watching over little Eve, I felt a chill and began to shiver, and sure enough, when I looked at the doorway, there stood my mother all glittery-eyed looking across the room at that baby. I knew what she intended to do. My little finger stuck out at an angle where she'd broken it so many times. She put her hands together as if she was praying, the way she always did before twisting my finger. I swooped that baby up. "You aren't going to hurt this child's hands!" I shouted at her.

Miss Anna's bedroom light went on, and I heard her coming down the hall, all quick like to the nursery, and my mother began to fade.

"What happened," she panted from coming so fast.

"That lady," I said, "she was here, looking at this child, and I told her she wasn't going to hurt this one, not this one." I held out my hand with the twisted little finger.

"Oh my God," Miss Anna said in a strange, unbelieving voice, as she took my hand in her gloved one. "Who did this to you?"

"My mama," I said.

"Your mother? Describe her, tell me about her," she insisted. I held the baby close and shut my eyes, thinking back. "My mama and I, well, we lived rough, never having a home or nothing. But we scrounged and made camps down by the river. She was a Mexican woman, small, very pretty, but down on her luck, and she never told me about her life before I came. I learned never to ask questions. She was awful interested in this here lot, and we watched the house being built, and then she slipped inside."

"She what?" Miss Anna said leaning toward me.

"She slipped inside, she got thinner and thinner and smaller and smaller, and then like vapor or a cloud, a white mist, she just slipped into the cellar."

"Have you seen her?" she asked.

"Not until tonight. Brige said there was a lady that came sometimes. I knew who it was, but I didn't see her until tonight."

By this time, Miss Anna was sitting down in the chair by the cradle. She breathed deep, and then she looked at me in a new way. "So you are the Chinee girl that Bess talked about."

"Bess?" I questioned.

"Yes, Bess was the woman who raised Narciste and me after… well after things happened. Then, our house burned down, and we went to live with papa and Charlotte in San Francisco, but Bess, she was like our first mother. See, our biological mother was a Mexican woman who hissed at us and twisted our hands. When the house burned down, she just walked away, but Bess saw her years after with a small Chinee girl. You know what this means?"

"Yes, I know now." And then Miss Anna, she started to cry.

"We must never let this child out of our sight," she sobbed.

"Yes," I nodded.

Chapter 9

Miss Anna

"The ways of the world are wondrous to behold," that's what Brige said when I told her the story the next morning. "What's that girl's name? We can't keep calling her the Chinee girl," she continued.

"I don't want to tell Narciste or Evelyn any of this," I told Brige. She agreed. Then I called the Chinee girl to the kitchen. "We can't call you Chinee girl anymore," I told her. "What is your real name? What did maman call you?"

"Rose Petal," she said softly. "She said I was as soft and pretty as rose petals when I was born, smelled like them too."

"Well, your new name is Rose Petal Gomez Duprey," I told her. "That's who you are from this day forth."

Narciste went to the City and stayed away a lot. I knew he liked to see papa and Charlotte, and I suspected that he had his own café au lait woman down there, but I never brought the subject up to him. I didn't want to know. Our half brother lived in Paris, and papa married Renee well. Only James was a mystery. He'd just disappeared, running away from papa's ranch in Chile. I knew that both papa and Charlotte grieved for him, and I knew that papa had men search him out, but no one was able to trace him at all.

Narciste stayed away because he didn't cotton to Evelyn, and he was ashamed at the way things happened. He took no interest in Eve, but he supported the household well, and us four women were happy in each other's presence.

And that bright little Eve, she was a darling baby. She did my heart good just to look at her. By the time she was three months old, she smiled and laughed at us when we spoke to her. Her little eyes darted here and there as if trying to figure us all out. We just loved that baby to death. We watched over her day and night, never allowing the lady near her. That lady, she began coming more and more often into that baby's room, but one of us mothers was always with that baby, guarding her.

Yes, the ways of the world are wondrous to behold. I just thought that every time I looked up to see Rose about the house or out in the garden tending to the vegetables and flowers. It was a miracle the way the fates, or the gods, or the spirits, I don't know who, had brought all of us together. Rose and I discussed the lady when Evelyn wasn't around. We didn't want to burden her although she knew the stories of a spook being in the house. The spook never appeared to her, but she believed the few things we said. But Evelyn, well, she had the kind of mind that put scary things to rest. She lived in the moment only, loving her child and being sweet to all of us.

She didn't do anything to help with the house; she assumed that was work only for Brige, Rose, or myself. She didn't read or play the piano or paint or visit friends or go to church. She lived quietly only engaged with her baby. Sometimes, her mother came to visit her, but Evelyn seemed uncomfortable during those visits. About the only thing she did was eat.

Lord, could that girl eat. She had been such a slim little thing the night of the Christmas party, so pretty, all decked out. And that awful thing happened with Narciste, and something happened to that girl's mind. It turned in on itself is what Brige said.

She was plump when she married, but she was pregnant. She continued to be plump after Eve was born, and then plump began to turn to fat. Just plain fat. The only time she wasn't munching on something was when Narciste returned from his business in San Francisco. When she holed up in her room like she was scared to death to come out. Narciste asked after her, and sometimes, he went to her room, but she would get so agitated, that he started staying away. About the time that Eve was ten months old, I tried to talk to her about her husband.

"Evelyn, you have a husband. You are a wife and a mother. You need to claim your place with Mr. Narciste rather than be just a shadow in his presence. You could have your say about the house. You could set up dinner parties for his business friends. You could preside over the next Christmas party. I wouldn't mind. You could be a help to Mr. Narciste," I told her.

But she looked at the floor. "No," she said. "Not now."

"Then when?" I asked.

"I don't know," she said.

"You're like a child in the house. Don't you want to be a woman, a grown-up, with responsibilities and a family life?"

"I have all I want as it is," she said. I never brought it up again. In a way, I understood because when papa had brought up the subject that it was time for me to marry, I protested.

"Just let me run Narciste's house," I told papa. "That's all I want." He finally agreed as did my brother. To have a man in my bed, to have children? I didn't want these things.

"Well, you got your mother's blood," papa said after one argument. I just couldn't get that pronouncement out of my head.

"I wonder if our mother felt like she was auctioned off?" I mused to Rose one day. "Maybe having that idea in her head is what turned her crazy when she had to marry and have children."

"You think she was crazy?" Rose asked squinting her eyes.

"Had to be… or is," I answered. "According to Bess, she hated Narciste and me, wished we were never born, almost let Narciste die when he was a baby, and look what she did to our hands? She crazy, all right."

"She hurt only my little finger," Rose said looking down at her hand. "Mostly she protected me, took care of me the best way that she could. When I asked why I was Chinee, she got the strangling crying and left for three days. There must have been something dramatic about my father, something she couldn't allow herself to think about. Could she have loved a Chinee man? You think that she could?"

"I don't know," I answered. "I wish Bess was still with us. She could probably have something to say about it. Bess, she seen everything. Nothing got past her."

I often thought about Bess, about the soft bosom of Charlotte when she hugged me to her, about Brige, Evelyn, and now Rose Petal. I thought about the goodness of these women.

My brother, Narciste, he made a lot of money. I knew because when he was in the house

Doing his books with his accountant, he would share his bank books with me. "We're worth a lot of money, Anna," he would say and sigh as if it was a burden. "I need a son to carry on when I can't anymore," and then he'd visit Evelyn's room, and I would hear them arguing and Evelyn crying. Narciste, he would stomp out of the house and not come back for days. Brige would cook something special for Evelyn, and she'd eat and eat, her fat moon-face looking entirely vague.

Then a time came when Narciste began looking at Rose Petal in the way that men have. Oh, I knew what he was thinking. He'd be working in his room and call down for Rose to bring his food up to him on a tray. I began to be afraid for her. And then one night Brige saw him sneaking down to the cellar room, and she told me about it the next morning.

I called Rose into the parlor. "Rose, you don't have to do anything Mr. Narciste asks you to do."

"Yes, ma'am," she said looking down at her apron.

"Now, you hear me, Rose?"

"Yes, I do," she said softly.

"Mr. Narciste, he a good man, a good provider, but it's the nature of men, you know, to want to do things with women. Do you know about those things, Rose?"

"I surely do," she said, looking over my shoulder and across the room as if she saw someone standing behind me.

The next time that Narciste in the house, I tole him that we had to have a talk. "Narciste, I know how you been looking at Miss Rose Petal," I told him. "Now, you can't do that anymore, you hear?"

"What's it to you?" he sneered at me.

"Because, Narciste, Miss Rose Petal is our sister," I said. He blanched white as store-bought sugar.

"What you saying?" he said in a scared voice.

"I says that she is our sister," I said in a matter-of-fact voice. "You wanna know how I know?"

He nodded and leaned back in his chair. And I began to unravel our family story as I had pieced it together.

Chapter 10

Mr. Narciste

I wish Anna hadn't tole me nothing about that Chinee girl, that Rose Petal one. God, I wish she hadn't tole me.

Chapter 11

Brige

If this ain't the strangest house I ever seen. It would be just my luck to come to work here. Oh, I could leave if I wanted to, could just collect my pay and skedaddle. But something holds me here; I feel like I am one of them. And that "lady"? She don't scare me none. I come from a place where ghosts are certain, spirits are everywhere, faeries live in the wild, and pookas play tricks. First time that lady came into my kitchen late at night where I was still setting up for the next day, I said, "Whata you want? Ain't gona harm me or any of the others in this house, you old haint. Now get away from me." She looked startled and left. I know she's around, but she hasn't come into my kitchen again.

And to think that she's the mother of Mr. Narciste, Miss Anna, and now Rose Petal. Strange things happen in this world, I swear. And speaking of strange things, there's Miss Evelyn to think about. I told Miss Anna she got all turned inside herself after what happened with Mr. Narciste, with that baby coming on and everything. I remember the night that her papa approached Mr. Narciste and the shouting and the slamming down of books and finally the call for the whiskey decanter and glasses. Then the next thing you know, Miss Anna and me, well, we're decorating for a wedding.

Miss Evelyn was as white as a ghost at that wedding. Didn't smile or nothing. She said what the priest told her to say, then she let Mr. Narciste kiss her on the cheek. Her mama looked as mad as a wet hen and criticized just everything from the bouquet of flowers on the table to the canapés on silver trays. Then she took Miss Evelyn up to the room where she would sleep. The arrangement was that it wasn't Mr. Narciste's room. She was to have her own because of her delicate condition. They were in that room a long time arranging things while the men got drunk below. Mr. Narciste? He got so drunk he couldn't make it up the stairs to his room or hers on that wedding night. Miss Anna and me lay him out on the sofa in the front parlor. The next day, he was pretty sick, but he asked me to pack his business bag like I always done, and he lit out for San Francisco. Didn't come back for a month.

They're really not married at all if you ask me. Not at all. Miss Anna don't think so either. But one good thing we got out of the situation, is that pretty little child. Our Eve.

And Jasus, Mary, and Joseph! Can that Evelyn eat. She gona get so big she won't be able to get through her bedroom door if she don't watch out. I swear, she eats three helpings of everything. Guess some of it's my fault because I know what she likes, and I cook special for her sometimes.

And then there's Rose. My, oh my, Miss Rose Petal. Now, Miss Anna's smart and organized and interested in sewing and books. She's got so many projects going at the same time. Evelyn eats and sleeps and plays with her baby. But that Rose, she kinda slinks around. Oh never in a bad way. She just sees what should be done and does it! Like the way she tends that garden out back. I could walk down its rows and not notice a thing. Miss Rose? She walks down the rows and sees a hundred things… "there's a good bug… oh oh, slug under that leaf, color of that plant not right, need more coffee grounds worked into the soil here." Where she got these ideas nobody knows, not even her. She says it's just a sixth sense she's always had. I wonder what she thinks when the Chinee gardeners come each week. That one old man right nice to our Rose. He smiles and pats her shoulder and nods his head up and down. There's young men, too, looking her over, but she pays them no mind. I wonder about that. It would be only natural if she took to one of them.

Well, it has to be her calling about men, just like it is for me and Miss Anna and I guess, even Miss Evelyn. After I saw my mother give birth to ten children and do more work than my Da ever did on our tiny holding in Donegal, I just said to myself that I sure didn't want a life like that.

I feel real protective of Rose. When I saw Mr. Narciste go down to that cellar one night, I about had a fit. He'd been looking at Rose. Looked at me that way when I first come here, but I just glinted my eyes at him as if to say "Keep your hands off. Don't think 'maid' means 'made'."

That's what my cousin taught me before I came here and went into service. So, I told Miss Anna about what I saw, and she pursed her lips, and said she'd see about that. It never happened again, and I watched like a hawk.

Guess that's my real job, watching this family like a hawk shopping for a rat. It is the job I was assigned the day I was born back in Donegal, to take care of some Creole people in California that can't take care of themselves.

Chapter 12

Rose Petal

Time comes when Grandpa Narciste and his Charlotte "they go to God," as Mr. Narciste says. Miss Anna and him, they went to the funeral in San Francisco both times, stayed with Charlotte's girl. Funny how they refer to her like that. Charlotte's boy is still in Europe. Sister says he's never coming back. And that James, well, he's gone for sure. Miss Anna brought a big, old trunk back from the last funeral trip filled with remembrances of her father and the family's New Orleans past.

Time comes when none of us in this house are moving as fast as we used to. All that is except Miss Eve. She's sixteen now, ready for a coming out party Mr. Narciste insists on giving her. But it won't be held in this house, oh no. Mr. Narciste rents a big, fancy room at the Senator Hotel. Miss Eve goes to the Lichtenstein Academy for

Young Women. She's real smart, can read just about anything. She's got lots of friends inviting her here and there, but she never invited anyone here… says it would upset her mama and Miss Anna. She's right about that.

Chapter 13

Miss Eve

Growing up in this house has been wonderful and horrible all at the same time. Wonderful because I have three mothers who worship the ground that I walk on, or that's what they've always told me. Even papa has come around. He began asking about my marks in school and giving me presents when I did well, which I always did. This is a big, comfortable house with plenty of nooks and crannies where I could invent castles and caves and hidey holes. It's a place where my imagination knew no constraints.

It's horrible because of the lady. She might just as well have sat right down at the dinner table with us each evening, she was so much a part of this family. Aunt Anna and Brige always said if she showed up in my room, I was to curl up my fists and shake them at her and tell her to "scat". But I never really saw her. Still when I would go to the hidey holes, a whisp of something would swish by me and I'd know that she'd been there. Aunt Anna and Brige made me promise that I'd never tell an outsider about her. And I never did. Well, there was Vivian, my childhood playmate from down the block, but that's another story.

Because of the lady, I never asked friends to come home with me from school, and Vivian wasn't allowed in my house either. Her mama wouldn't allow it because of what the lady did to Vivian's hands when she was a small child. I can remember my papa and her mother having an argument in the parlor, and after she left, I saw him pacing and pulling at his hair and asking Aunt Anna what to do and Aunt Anna saying "Pay her off as usual, Narciste," whatever that meant. Papa visited Vivian's mother a lot, or that's what Vivian told me when we played together at school or when I went to play in her backyard.

Sometimes, I would invite someone from school like Hattie Donahue to have sandwiches and tea in the gazebo in the garden when the weather was warm. Brige kept an eye on us and Rose would be working in the garden. I told Hattie that Rose was my auntie just like Aunt Anna, but Hattie said that it wasn't possible for a white girl to have a Chinese relative. I just looked over at Rose weeding the pansy bed. What did Hattie Donahue know anyway?

Then there was my mother as big as a house. The one thing that my mother loved was listening to her stories on the radio. When I was a little girl, I can remember curling up beside her on her bed and listening to the stories all afternoon. I thought the radio was filled with real little people, and mama just laughed at me.

I talked to papa about going to a women's college in Oakland when I left high school, but he wasn't too keen on it. It wasn't a matter of money. He just said the house would be empty without me. But right before graduation, something happened to change all that. The lady did appear to me for the first time. I awoke choking and hardly able to breathe. She stood beside my bed holding onto a man's leather belt which she'd wrapped around my neck and she was pulling it tight, like a noose. I grabbed at it, wrestled it out of her hands, ripped it off my throat, but then she grabbed my hands and began twisting my fingers. I heard the bones crack. I screamed and screamed, and the whole household came running, even my mother lumbered out of her room. "She did it," Aunt Anna cried to papa as Brige ran for ice to wrap up my hands. Papa told me to drink a tumbler of brandy, and I don't remember much after that.

The next day, I heard Miss Rose crying in the kitchen. "We watched her so careful," she sobbed to Brige, "so careful." It took a long time for my splintered fingers to heal, but they ended up all crooked like Aunt Anna's. She taught me how to wear lace gloves, and everybody was real sad for a long time. I never went back to school.

One by one, I lost my family, first papa, then Aunt Anna, my mother, and the last was Brige. Only Miss Rose remained to take care of the house and me, and she was old, old, old! I know that the night my hands got broken, so did my mind in a way, just as everybody's mind that lived in that house was hurt in some way. Papa said Grandpa Narciste warned him about building a house on that lot, and at the end of his life, papa admitted that his father had been right.

I lived out my days like a haint in the house not so different from the lady. And then the night came when she appeared again with the belt in her hand, jerked me

Chapter 14

One More Time

Exactly a week after my first visit with Mrs. Gentry, I arrived at Happy Retreat House and asked for her again. Mrs. Conneally was called. "I'm sorry," she said, "Mrs. Gentry died last night."

"Oh my God, I'm so sorry," I said in a stunned voice. "I just talked to her a week ago, and she seemed so spry and everything. Was she ill?"

"No," Mrs. Conneally said with a sigh, "just very old. She just went to sleep. The morning staff went into rouse her for breakfast and she was gone."

"Oh, again, I am so sorry," I said not knowing what to do next. "She just seemed so full of life and in good health, well except for her fingers, of course, the arthritis and all."

"Arthritis?" Mrs. Conneally said. "Well, yes, arthritis had set in, but her hands had been crippled in some kind of accident when she was a little child."

I turned to go. Her hands? An accident? What had Mrs. Gentry left out of her story the week before?

I left Happy Retreat House and went downtown to the County Building and the Recorder's Office. "I want to look up the ownership of Number Ten Twenty-second Street," I told the clerk. She looked at me strangely for a moment. "It is public information, right?" I asked her.

"Oh yes," she said and went into the back room. She was gone quite some while. When she finally returned with a big fat book of ancient description, she tiredly lay it down before me. "This is the original book which describes the lots when Twenty-second Street was laid out," she said. "There is no Number Ten. It's skipped. There's lot nine and eleven, but no ten. I don't know why."

"Can I look up ownership by providing the original family name that built the house?" I asked. Her look told me that I was annoying her. She had better things to do with her day.

"John?" she called back into the stacks. "I need some help here." A bespectacled young man emerged.

"Yes?" he said smiling. I told him about my search and what we had turned up so far which was nothing. Yet, right there on Twenty-second Street stood a large Italianate house which according to two sources had been there since 1910. I knew the name of the original family who owned the property. Could we trace the property that way?

He said he thought we could. All the property records from even the earliest days were on the computer now, and he'd give them a squint. He took me into another office where he settled in front of a computer. I sat beside him.

"Now give me the names," he said. "Narciste Duprey, hmmm," he said scrolling up and down various lists. "Gosh, there's nothing at all."

"Try Anna Duprey, or Eve Duprey, or even Velvulotta Duprey," I told him. He typed in the various names, he clicked various sites, but he found nothing.

"This doesn't make sense," I said. "Property taxes? Somebody must have paid property taxes over the years. Can you check that?"

"Oh yes," he said, "different site, but this should do it." And with a few clicks and scrolls, he began checking the address and the names again. But there was nothing.

"There is a big house sitting between Nine and Eleven on Twenty-second Street," I said. "It's been there for over one hundred years. It's real, but there's no record of it at all or of the people that lived there?" The young man shrugged his shoulders. "I wish that I could have been more help," he said very unconcerned. I thanked him and left the office.

Three days later I attended Mrs. Gentry's funeral. I sat at the back of Ryans Mortuary. Her elderly children, middle-aged grandchildren, and a few great grandchildren sat in the front four rows. No one paid any attention to me, even when I stood behind them at the Old Sacramento Cemetery for the graveside prayers. I left before they did.

A few months later, I revisited the gravesite. A headstone had been placed. When I looked at the name, I was shocked. Vivian Duprey Gentry, 1901-2000. Duprey? Her maiden name was Duprey? Why hadn't she told me that when she related the stories about the Hoffstaters, the Jensons, and Mookie Sonnenberg?

A year passed, but I never forgot Mrs. Gentry. Sometimes, I went to her grave in the cool of a Sacramento evening just to sit there and ask questions. One evening, I felt that I wasn't alone. Someone lingered nearby. Was it a grandchild come to honor her? I saw the swish of a long skirt out of the corner of my eye.

I decided to move along. I walked casually down the gravel path between old plots until I came to a big stone Seraphim. I slid behind it and turned to look back at Mrs. Gentry's grave, and there was a shimmering in the air. Then a young Chinese woman materialized, her soft long skirt rippling by the breeze, her long black hair hanging down her back. She raised one hand to move a dark hank of hair from her face. She stood there for some time, and then kissing her fingers, she touched them to the gravestone, and quietly left, becoming nothing as the distance swallowed her.

I walk past that house still and stop and gaze at it. I wonder if Miss Velvulotta still walks its halls, enters and exits the rooms, slides down to the cellar? What other spirits might live there? And what would happen to anyone who tried to open up that house again, the House of the Broken Hands.

About the Author

Barbara O'Donnell is a story teller, writer, and teacher who lives in Midtown, Sacramento, California. She established Pusheen Press in 2000 and a list of publications can be seen in this book and on her web site, celticgirlswriteon.com.

A Conversation with the Author

What's in a neighborhood walk, and how does it contribute to the building of a story? In this case, my neighborhood walk put me on a street where an empty mansion sat. I became curiouser and curiouser about the house, and why nobody lived in it. I watched it carefully for about ten years. It remained empty, no lights on, no car in the driveway, drapes closed. But somebody was maintaining the small ivy-covered yard, and a sprinkler system watered during the hot summer months. What on earth was the history of the house?

I could have gone to the plat books in the property division of the city and looked up the address to see who owned the property, but I never got around to it. Instead, I walked past and wondered.

And then one day, it occurred to me that the reason no one lived in the house was that it was haunted! Yes, haunted. That would explain things. But who haunted it? What ghost lingered there? And what had happened in the house so that a ghost couldn't find eternal rest, but remained in her earthly abode. Her. Yes, I was quite sure it was a her, a she-ghost.

Had there been a murder in the house? A suicide? That was too ordinary. A million books had been written with this the theme of the story. It had something to do with life a hundred and fifty years ago here in Sacramento, and a woman who hated her plight in life. "I'm not a brood mare," I heard her voice saying. "I hate the fact that you married me only to have children to carry on your name." But in fact, that is exactly what had happened. This woman produced children whom she hated and refused to nurse. Someone intervened on their behalf. They lived and thrived. But the woman took her revenge on those children in a simple yet painful way, and that's what locked her out of heaven.

And so the story took shape in my imagination. Voices came to me even as I walked past the house. Voices came to me in the middle of the night when I couldn't sleep, each telling their story. I heard their accents, saw them in their historical setting, wondered at their lives, and finally, began writing. And that's how a simple neighborhood walk created story, story which was to become *The House of the Broken Hands.*

The creative process is so magical. You can't explain it with logic. You can't plan it with outline. Eventually, the writer uses skills in the left brain to organize the images coming out of the right brain. But the metaphor of the muse always speaks through the imaginative right brain before engaging with the old language-skill-center left brain.

How does it happen, this magical idea? It comes out of vision, hearing a noise for the first or hundredth time, sniffing at an interesting smell, feeling a texture that intrigues. And then those senses bring up pictures of other times, conversations with other people, feelings based on literal experiences, observations of what makes people tick, the enterprising behavior of a pet, the saying of a grandmother. And all of a sudden a new world of story is created with characters and a plot of events, and if you're lucky, a conclusion.

Or it may begin with just a lone face looking at you, a lone sound repeating itself endlessly, such as the crack of a whip or the melody of a music box, a truck backfiring. It may begin with the smell of a turkey roasting making you remember a special or horrific Thanksgiving. You may touch the satin of a garment and remember that special dress that your aunt made you for the holidays. Something coming out of your senses brings up images and remembrances and you begin to tell a story.

Many times you have no idea where the story is going and you bumble along until it becomes clear. How much time does that take? Hours, days, or sometimes years. But as a writer you are compelled to continue playing with the ideas and images until a story is finished. Sometimes you're lucky because the whole story comes at once, and you have a hard time getting the words down fast enough. And sometimes, story comes out of a dream, a dream of such force that it doesn't evaporate when awakening, but it is as solid as the covers pulled up to your chin.

Once I got a half story in the middle of the night. It was only after I wrote it down and read and reread it, that the other half became obvious, and I could finish it. Once, I heard the first four lines of a poem so clearly that I wrote them down immediately and then like a spool unwinding, line after line came to me, until 25 of them stared back at me from the page. Once, after hearing a friend say that I should write a novel after reading a short travelogue I had written about a trip to Ireland, I began trying to tell a story based on my journals at that time. It took ten years of writing, rewriting, sorting everything out, changing the narrator's voice, changing the character's names back and forth, adding new characters who became part of a complicated plot, and trying to get my final narrator "out of the shadows" and into the bright sunlight of story.

So, there you have it. The creative process.

There are several things I find interesting about the process. First, I'll never forget a seminar on creativity I attended. The presenter told us, "You don't say someday I'll be a writer. You say I am a writer. It has already happened. Perhaps I need to develop my skills. Perhaps I have to gain experience. But it isn't a someday thing. It is now. You are a writer or a sculptor or musician or chef." That idea changed my life.

Secondly, I find it fascinating that in talking to people who flock to writing workshops and seminars, who want to hear what the gurus have to say, only have one question during the Q and A's, and that is, "How do we get published?" But when you inquire about their work, you find that only about a third of them actually write! They've dabbled in writing. They have a great idea for a novel, but write on a continuous, daily basis? Nope. Never happens.

You may have the muse whispering in your ear, but if you don't hone your craft by writing every day, the voice begins to recede, grow faint, says, "Why should I bother?" If you are a serious writer, you write. There is no way out. And every day that you write whether in a journal or a letter to a friend or a blog or a flash fiction or a 20 line poem, you are following your bliss as Joseph Campbell said. You are a writer who writes. Perhaps you will never be published by an outside company. Perhaps you don't like the idea or have the resources to self publish. It doesn't matter. You are a writer who writes. Eventually, the "hows" of sharing your work will come to you, and you'll know what to do. But you can never get to this stage if you are not a writer who writes.

And now back to the House of the Broken Hands. Because I was a writer, I wrote, following where my imagination led me. I studied the closed up house. I heard the voices of the characters who arrived onto my paper as if by magic. I untangled their voices, put together the pieces of their stories, and eventually, finished telling their family tale. This is a fictitious story, that is, very likely, true!

Q and A's

Q: How long did it take to write this bookeen, and what is a bookeen, anyway?
A: First, a bookeen is a little book, something we used to call a novella. It is too long for a short story, and not long enough for a novel. The ending "een" in Irish means "little", so I coined the term for a story of this length. There are some longer stories that fit together in a collection just fine, but there are some, like this one, that need to stand alone. Hence, the bookeen. It took about two years to work out this story from the time the idea came to me until the last revision.

Q: Why did you write about New Orleans people coming to California?
A: I've always had a particular interest in Louisiana and especially New Orleans culture and have read extensively about their respective histories. It seemed an interesting event that a gentleman from the old culture and his slaves would enter the rough and tumble time of the California

Gold Rush when the first wave of miners passed, and the entrepreneurs entered the town. And in the new society free blacks could take their place in the society. The restraints of the old culture could meld with the new, i.e. nobody knew you and you could live out your life as you pleased even when this meant a partnership with your former slaves.

Q: Why did you include a Mexican woman and Chinese man in the story?
A: I liked the idea that the marginalized should be part of this family history. It wasn't just a black and white thing. Mexicans had lost their status, land, and way of life after the area of California became part of the U.S. The Chinese were a despised minority. It seemed interesting that Velvulotta, the outcast in a sense, would find passionate relationship with another outcast.

Q: Why broken hands?
A: Velvulotta has no power. She can't do a big thing to get back at Narciste. How could she abuse her children in a small way? Not nursing them didn't work as Bess was and/ or found a wet nurse. But what sly way could this woman disfigure and hurt these children? That's when the idea came to me...she could break their little hands, a very insidious, cruel thing to do.

Q: Why did you include a California Indian woman warrior in Velvulotta's past?
A: Actually, I stole the idea from Isabelle Allende. I liked the DNA connection of an abused strong woman, gone

mad because of the cruelty done to her, passing down that madness to a great granddaughter.

Q: Narciste seems like an honorable man, but Little Narciste seems like a womanizer who uses and discards if he can.
A: I'll let the reader figure this out! Did he listen to his father about building the new house on the property? No. Did his mother's cruelty and disappearance affect his view of women as people to be used and discarded? Probably. Yet, he retains his protective affection for his sister, a redeeming virtue.

Q: Why are three generations affected in this story?
A: I've always been interested in family patterns, and in this case, the ghost dominates the house continuing with her revenge right down to the modern period when Mookie Sonnenberg is psychologically maimed by her appearance.

Q: Was it difficult to get the language of the characters right, the grammar, the patterns of words?
A: Yes, this took several revisions based on research and the way other authors "got it right" in their novels. First, I wrote the stories in standard English, but I quickly realized that I had to enable the characters to tell their stories in their own language patterns.